CLARISSA WILD

DESCRIPTION

Thrown out onto the streets by her mother after a surprise pregnancy, Emilia's life has been full of hardship and turmoil.

But when she's about to give up on life itself, a dangerously handsome stranger saves her from despair and brings her into his home to show her how to take back control ...

And how to burn for him.

BURN is dark mafia romance prelude novella to SICK BOYS. Contains disturbing content that might not be suitable for all readers.

DEDICATION

For all my girlies who have had to make the most
difficult decision in life.

I see you.

ONE

Emilia

I stare at the stick lying on the sink in front of me, my body feeling numb to the core.

My pupils dilate, and my heart begins to throb in my chest.

It's as if the walls of this grimy bathroom are caving in on me. Like the ground underneath my feet split open and threatens to devour me whole.

Two lines.

That's all it takes to destroy my world.

What I thought was just a bloated feeling these past few

weeks and nausea from eating some bad food turns out to be a whole different kind of thing. A child … growing inside me.

I plant my hand against my belly and touch my skin, suddenly feeling cold to the bone. I gaze up at the girl in the mirror, the girl whose eyes fill with tears.

This wasn't supposed to happen.

It was just supposed to be a one-time thing.

I'm only nineteen. How am I supposed to raise a child?

"Emilia! Get down here. Dinner's ready," my mom's shrill voice pulls me from my thoughts.

I swallow and rub away the tears, trying not to think about the human growing inside me while I turn and make my way downstairs.

My mother is already sitting at the table, throwing sloppy, hastily made stew into a bowl before she sits down to eat without waiting for me.

She gazes up when I quietly sit down and grab the spoon.

"Kinda late, don't you think?" she says.

"Sorry," I mutter, my voice mousy. Quiet. Like I'm supposed to be around her.

"You'd better be grateful for that food," she growls, slurping the stew like it's her last meal.

I nod as I pour some into a bowl. "I am. Thank you."

She gazes up at me again, her eyes searching my face like she's trying to find the lie.

"Your face is red," she mutters.

I stop and look down at the stew, which smells so nice even though I know she can't cook. Any food is better than none.

"Have you been crying?" she asks with a condescending tone.

"No, no," I say, laughing it off. "The water was just hot."

She puts down her spoon and stares at me. "You *have* been crying."

I don't know what to say. "I … I…"

She slams her fist onto the table, and I jolt up and down in my seat. "Don't lie to me!" She points at me like I'm a criminal in need of punishment. "I see the tearstains on your face."

She pauses, waiting for me to give her a reason, but I don't want to give them to her.

"Tell me why," she says through gritted teeth. "Is it because of that fucker Dean?"

I quickly shake my head.

"You know it's thanks to him we have food on the table right now," she adds, taking another bite with her spoon.

I clutch myself, staring at the food. "I know."

"No, I don't think you do. You're crying your eyes up there, and for what? It's not like he's going to see those tears." She takes another big bite. "What do you even want? You want a hug? You know they don't fix anything."

"I'm fine," I say, rubbing my belly with my hand.

"I give you food. Clothes. A roof over your head," she

mutters. "It's about time you showed a little g—"

Suddenly, she stops eating. Her eyes travel down to my hands.

And it's as if the blood leaves her skin.

Oh God.

She stands.

I do too.

We stare at each other for a moment. Then she rushes upstairs before I can.

"No! Mom, wait!" I scream as I try to catch up with her.

Too late. She's already opened the bathroom door and ran inside faster than I could chase her upstairs. Her hand clutches the stick, almost breaking it in two as she glares at me, her eyes almost spewing fire.

"You're pregnant?!"

"I only just found out," I mutter.

"I don't fucking care!" she screams. "I told you not to get pregnant!" She throws the stick at me. "What are we supposed to do now, huh?"

"I don't know," I say, tears welling up in my eyes.

"You're going to cost me everything I ever worked for!" Her face turns red from the screaming.

Redder than mine ever was, despite crying my eyes out only moments ago.

"A baby? Really?" she says. "You think I have the money to feed another one?"

"Can't you help me?" I ask. "We can think of something, right?"

"Help?" she screeches, shaking her head. "I've helped you so goddamn much already." She picks up a piece of my clothing and throws it at me. "Every fucking time you fuck up, I have to clean up the mess."

"Mom…"

"No, I'm done," she yells, picking up more dirty pieces and throwing them all at me. "I'm done helping you, I'm done with teaching you, I'm done with *everything!*"

"Please." My whole body is shaking. "Don't do this."

"Get out," she says, her low tone completely devoid of any emotion.

More tears well up in my eyes.

"I don't have anywhere to go," I say.

"I don't care!" she replies. "I'm *not* dealing with another fucking baby." She shoves me away. "Now get. Out."

I pick up the clothes and clutch them close, desperate for something to hug.

"But I can fix this," I mutter.

"No, you can't!" she says. "It's illegal. Did you forget the fucking news? It's not allowed here anymore. And I'm not going to go down for your mistake. Not again."

Again? I've never been pregnant before.

Unless she means … giving birth to me.

She pushes me so hard, I have to grab ahold of the staircase railing to stop myself from falling.

"Leave!" she shrieks madly.

I turn and run down the stairs, terrified she might throw me down if I don't go faster.

The scent of food fills my nostrils, but I push my hunger away and head straight for the front door.

"And don't you ever think of coming back again!" she yells as I shut the door behind me, blinking away the tears that keep coming. "You hear me? Leave me alone!"

I run out into the streets, as far away from the house as possible without looking back.

I can't stomach the thought of looking, let alone thinking about the home I left behind.

I didn't have much, but the room I slept in was mine. The clothes I wore were mine. The tiny bear I had was mine.

I didn't even have the time to grab any of it before she kicked me to the curb.

After a while, my legs begin to hurt, but I keep running until it begins to rain. My clothes slowly get soaking wet until I don't even have that anymore.

I drop them somewhere near a store and keep running.

They'll only drag me down. I don't know where I'm going or what I'll do next.

All I know is that I couldn't stay there for a minute longer.

God, I tried. I tried so long, so hard to live according to her rules, but even that wasn't enough.

I pause when I finally find an alley that doesn't look like a place where criminals meet. I huddle in the corner, hugging my legs for comfort because no one else ever would.

***

Vincenzo

I lean back against the car seat while the driver turns left and check my phone. Six days until my next scheduled meeting. Fifty-two minutes spent in the previous conversation. Two minutes too many.

I shake my head. That won't happen again.

My time is precious, and every minute wasted minute is one too many. Especially on those lot.

My fingers tighten around the phone.

There's another private message, but I ignore it and stuff my phone back into my pocket, then turn to look out the window. Gazing at the people going about their regular day-to-day life always calms me. It's the fact that it's quiet. Without any need to respond or smile at passersby. Like a cocoon I've enveloped myself in while I journey from one place to another. And there is absolutely nothing that I can do except sit back and enjoy.

Until my eyes land on a peculiar girl huddled in a corner between two apartment buildings.

"Stop," I command my driver.

"Sir?" he mutters. "You never—"

I glare at him through the rearview mirror until he swallows and immediately stops the car near the side of the road.

"Stay here and wait for me," I say before I open the car door and hop out.

The streets are filled with trash and mud, and I skip over a puddle in disgust. Even an ounce of that type of gunk on my shoes makes me want to hurl. But when I spot the girl again, I forget about caring and walk over to her.

She's not even remotely aware of my presence as I walk up to her, despite the fact that I tower over her and block the streetlights. Rain pitter-patters down onto the pavement and my clothes, which would normally annoy the shit out of me. But right now, all I can focus on is the soft sobs emanating from the girl just a few inches away from me.

Finally, she tilts her head ever so slightly, and her eyes immediately land on my boots. Slowly, they creep up my fitted pants and Colbert until her beautiful brown eyes connect with mine.

Her pupils dilate, and she gasps in shock. "Who are you?" She leans back. "What do you want?"

I cock my head while I crouch and extend a hand. "Vincenzo Ricci."

Her eyes flick back and forth from my face to my hand, her lip twitching with distrust.

"I'm here to help," I add.

She narrows her eyes. "Why?"

A smile creeps onto my face.

In this world, a healthy amount of skepticism is necessary to survive.

She's smart.

"Because you look like you need it," I reply.

She frowns and wipes a wet strand of hair off her face. "I don't need help."

I look her up and down. She's barely wearing any clothes, and all of it is soaking wet. She's clutching herself like she needs someone to hug but has no one left.

"You're on your own in an alley, completely soaked through, crying your eyes out," I say, lifting a brow. "It's okay not to be strong for a day."

She gazes at me but doesn't inch back when I try to get closer.

"C'mon," I say, beckoning her. "Let me get you somewhere warm and safe."

She looks at my hand and then scans my face, almost as if she's trying to spot the lie.

"You can leave anytime you want," I add. "You can trust me."

Her eyes flicker with hope.

She takes in a breath.

Finally, her hand reaches for mine.

The smile on my face grows when her skin touches mine, her fingers fitting so neatly into the palm of my hand. And when I rise, lifting her up too, I stop only to stare at how gorgeous she truly is. Her long black hair sticks to her porcelain face, her soft, heart-shaped lips, those round, hooded eyes staring straight into my soul … all of it beguiles me.

I pull her forward, out of the shadows of the alley and into the open. The rain still pours down on us, but my driver quickly hops out of the car and fetches an umbrella from the back, rushing to us.

"Sir, your new Colbert will get wet!" he says, huddling close to us to keep us dry.

"I don't care," I say as I guide her toward the car.

She seems unsure of me, and I completely understand why.

Who would ever trust a stranger whisking you off the streets?

Trust is a dangerous thing, only extended to those we deem most worthy. But I will prove myself to her.

"Open the door," I command my driver when we get to the car.

"Sir, are you sure we should be—"

I throw him a damning look.

Just one simple glance is enough to make him suck in the air.

"Yes, sir." He swiftly pulls it open and waits for us, holding up the umbrella so we don't get wet any further than we already are.

It won't help her clothes, but at least it'll give her the one thing she lost on her way to this alley: her dignity.

And I cannot fucking wait to restore it to its original state.

I slide in first and pat down on the couch, watching her contemplate her options.

"Get in," I tell her.

She bites down on her bottom lip and looks around the street.

I didn't lie. She's free to go wherever she wants, whenever she wants. I won't stop her. I won't go after her if she chooses to flee right now and never look back, and I wouldn't blame her if she did.

But what I'm offering is something far more valuable than the outside world can ever give her: A new start.

To me, this girl seems like an intricate puzzle.

And I can't fucking wait to unlock everything she has to hide.

TWO

Emilia

I can't believe I'm going along with this stranger, hopping into his expensive-looking car and letting him take me wherever he wants.

It's dumb. Insane.

But it's too late to stop it now as the car has already begun to drive.

My body feels frozen, and I don't know if it's from the cold rain soaking through my clothes or from this man whose warm, callused hand I can still feel wrapped around my fingers even though it's no longer there.

I stare at my hand, afraid to throw even one glance.

But I can see him look my way through the left side of my eyes. "Do I frighten you?"

I rub my lips together and shake my head.

He snorts and smiles softly.

Fuck.

Of course he can see right through my posturing.

I push through my anxiety and turn to look at him, but I'm struck in awe at how handsome he truly is. His chiseled jaw with a neatly trimmed beard, that short, textured salt-and-pepper hair with a low fade, buff arms barely contained in that Colbert of his, the intricate tattoos snaking up from his hand all the way to his wrist hiding underneath his clothes, and those piercing blue eyes with a smoldering gaze that reminds me of the moon in the night sky.

Simply breathtaking.

Those eyes will make me do things I'll regret.

A blush spreads on my cheeks, and I quickly look away again.

He must be twice my age.

My hands tighten across my waist. I cannot let my guard down, no matter what.

"It's okay," he says.

Suddenly, I feel a tickle near my neck. Gently sliding across my skin, his finger pushes a strand of hair behind my ear.

"Most people are intimidated by me."

I shudder against the lavish leather seat.

His hand leaves my skin, and so does the warmth that filtered through my body, goose bumps erupting all over.

I throw another glance at him. I don't even know what I'm thinking going along with this. But I was in such a low place there that I couldn't resist taking him up on the offer when he took my hand, even though I know it's dangerous.

My mother taught me to be wary of any and all men.

Especially the ones who make too many promises.

But what value do her words have now that she threw me out onto the streets?

"I won't hurt you," he says. "If that's what you're worried about."

"I'm not," I lie, glancing over at him once more, even though his killer looks make it so damn hard. But I can't afford to look weak, despite my obvious low. If there's anything I know about this world, it's that people love to take advantage of those in a bad spot.

"If you want to stop the car, you can tell me, and I'll drop you off. No questions asked," he adds.

"I'm fine," I reply, licking my lips. "I just want to know why you would take me with you?"

A coarse, thin smile forms on his face. "Because I saw you hunched over in that alley. Crying." His fingertips reach for my face, but he stops right before he touches my cheek. "I can't resist helping occasionally."

"So you do this often? Take in girls off the streets?"

He laughs and shakes his head. "Not often, no. But I have helped people before."

People. I wonder who.

Judging from the brand of this car, the suit he's wearing, and the driver in front of us, he's got loads and loads of cash to dish out. Which means he's either a businessman or a criminal. Knowing my track record, probably the second.

But can I really say no to help when I have nothing at all and no one else to go to?

"I've given you my name, but you still haven't told me yours," he says, breaking my train of thought.

"I, uh … Emilia." I don't want to give my last name just yet.

Who knows what he intends to do.

Suddenly, my stomach roars, and I rub my hand along my side to stop the noise. But when I turn my head, he's looking at me with that raised brow and a filthy smirk on his face, and I know he heard.

Goddammit.

"You're hungry."

Not a question. A statement.

"I'm f—"

He snaps his finger at his driver. "Take us to Pierre's."

"Yes, sir," the driver responds.

"What's Pierre's?" I ask, confused.

"A restaurant," Vincenzo replies. "One that serves the best dishes this city has to offer."

Pierre as in … Pierre Faveurre?! The most expensive restaurant in this city?

I swallow. Now I'm sure he's loaded.

19

"No, no, wait," I mutter. "I can't go there."

"Why not?" He sounds so calm even though the place he just suggested is so out of reach to people like me, but like it's the most normal thing in the world to him.

"I-I'm not dress—"

"I'll get you a dress," he says, and he grabs my hand and brings it to his lips, pressing a soft kiss to the top. "Everything's on me today."

I'm too flabbergasted to know how to respond.

He snaps his fingers again. "Quick stop at Nalaga first."

Nalaga? Outfits there cost at least a thousand a piece, if not more.

"Yes, sir," the driver responds, and he makes a quick turn to the left.

I don't know what to say, it's all a bit too much. And within seconds, we've already arrived.

The car stops, and Vincenzo steps out, only to open my door for me like a real gentleman. And I don't know what I did to deserve all this … or if it's all a trap.

Vincenzo holds out his hand. "C'mon."

I reluctantly take it and let him guide me into the big, intricately designed building. There's a red carpet welcoming the customers, along with rows and rows of closets filled with lavish dresses, all carrying cards with dizzying numbers on them.

"Pick any you like," he says, releasing my hand.

"There are so many …" I mutter.

"Do you want them all?"

My eyes widen. He sounds like he means it. Literally.

"This one looks nice," I say, and I grab a long purple dress that's one of the cheaper ones.

He scratches his chin and raises a brow. "You sure, or are you just picking that one because it costs the least?"

I grin and push the blush away. "I like it."

"Can I help you?" a lady at the front desk asks as she approaches us. She lowers her nose at me in that same way rich people usually do when they spot me. My drenched clothes definitely give away that I don't belong in a place like this.

Vincenzo steps forward, blocking her from coming to me. "Dressing room."

The woman swallows and stares him up and down. "And who will be paying for that outfit?"

"I will," he snarls.

She huffs but eventually caves. "All right. Dressing room's that way." She points me in the right direction.

"Thank you," I say under my breath as I carefully grab the purple dress off the railing.

Vincenzo grabs my wrist, stopping me. His smoldering eyes are directed only at the lady who runs the store. "She said 'thank you.'"

"It's fine," I mutter under my breath.

"No," he responds in a calm but threatening manner. "She disrespected you."

The way he looks at her almost makes me want to say a prayer for her.

Who really is this man?

The lady looks embarrassed, and she quickly steps back. "You're welcome. Take your time."

Vincenzo's lip twitches until the woman finally spins on her heels and returns to the front desk register.

Just one look already made her scurry off like a scared little mouse.

Who has that kind of power?

A dangerous man.

I clutch the dress close and quietly walk to the dressing room, not taking a breath until I've locked myself inside.

Oh my God. What are you even doing, Emilia?

What were you thinking going along with a man like that?

He could do all sorts of things to you, and no one would ever find out!

But it's too late to turn back now. He's right outside this room, waiting for me to put on this dress and see if it fits.

I take a deep breath and start undressing. No point in delaying the inevitable. Though, when I slide the fabric over my skin, I'm surprised by how well it fits.

I chuck my wet clothes onto the wooden chair in the back and open the door when I'm ready. The glinting look in his eyes catches me off guard as they swoop over my body from head to toe, his tongue dipping out to lick the top of his lip.

"Gorgeous," he says.

And just that one word makes my skin erupt into goose bumps.

Compliments from random strangers have never made

me want to blush. And I don't understand why I so easily go with everything he says and does.

He has this kind of charm about him that's impossible to ignore.

But it also makes it hard to defy him.

"Almost like it was made just for you," he adds, making me smile.

He makes me feel something I haven't felt in a long while … like I'm actually pretty.

But I feel like I'm only playing pretend. "I could never pay for this," I reply.

"You don't need to," he says, and he walks to the desk. "The lady wants to continue wearing it."

"Of course," the woman at the desk responds, rolling her eyes.

"She left her old clothes in the dressing room. Dispose of them, if you will," he says. "Put it on the tab." Vincenzo puts down his card. "Take ten percent off the dress's price."

She eyes him down.

"Or do you want me to tell your supervisor how poorly you treated one of his biggest customers?"

She swallows again. "Of course, sir. Ten percent off it is." She hastily enters it into the machine on the desk, then grabs his card and swipes it. "Thank you, sir. Would you like the receipt?"

"Keep it." Vincenzo makes his way over to me and holds out his hand. "Ready?"

I'm still too stunned to even know how to reply to all of

these random acts of kindness, but also because I just don't trust what's going on.

Who would help a random girl off the streets?

What does he gain by doing all this?

But when his hand folds into mine, I still let him pull me back out onto the street, wearing this fancy, overpriced dress that I would never be able to wear if it wasn't for him.

The driver opens the car door again, and I step inside. Vincenzo scoots in behind me, and the driver shuts the door.

"You seem overwhelmed," Vincenzo says, breaking the spell of silence between us.

I shrug. "It's just that … I'm not used to this kind of …"

"Kindness?" he fills in for me.

I nod. "That, but also this kind of lifestyle."

He snorts. "Lifestyle. Money isn't a lifestyle. It's a tool." He makes a fist. "A weapon."

I gulp.

Weapons … to strike who?

"But it also allows me to give to people in need," he says, relaxing his muscles again when he turns to look my way. "To help those who others have abandoned."

I lower my eyes. "I wasn't…"

"You weren't what?"

"Never mind." I look out the window.

Telling him everything there is to know about me would be foolish. Not to mention dangerous.

"My mom's waiting for me at home," I blurt out. Just to be safe.

When I look at him, all he does is grin. "I'm sure she is."

Well, that didn't nearly sway him as much as I had hoped it would.

"I'm still going to take you to dinner," he says as the car comes to a stop.

I frown, confused why this random, rich stranger would go through all this trouble just for me.

"If you'll let me, of course," he adds, cocking his head in that same attractive way he did before when I first saw him.

My stomach growls again, answering for me, and he laughs a little. "I think that's a yes."

The driver opens the doors again. "I've booked a table for you, sir."

"Thank you," Vincenzo replies, and he holds out his arm for me. "Will you join me?"

With a tentative smile, I scoot out of the car. I feel like Cinderella, who just got taken to the ball after getting a dress made by the fairy godmother herself.

Vincenzo guides me up a couple of staircases to where a man guards the front door. When he sees us, he immediately opens the doors. "Mr. Ricci, right this way, sir."

"They've been expecting you," I whisper as another server shows us to the table.

"They know me, and I know them," he replies.

I look up into his brilliant eyes. "You seem to know an awful lot of people."

"Out of necessity, not because I enjoy it," he says, as the server scoots my chair back and shows me where I'm seated. "But I do enjoy this."

I sit down. "This?"

He pushes my chair forward and sits down opposite me. "Having dinner with a girl like you."

"And what kind of girl is that?"

The server hands us the menus, and the prices make me dizzy, just like in the clothing store.

"Would you like something to drink?" the server asks.

"Chateau Lafite," Vincenzo replies. "The bottle."

The server walks off, leaving us alone again.

And I can't stop staring at just how handsome this guy looks, like a Greek god sculpted from stone.

"So … why were you there in that alley?" he suddenly asks, catching me off guard.

"Oh, I … had an argument back home that was pretty bad," I say. It's not a lie, but it's not the entire truth, either.

"With your mother?" he asks.

I nod. "It happens."

"A lot?"

My eyes narrow. "Why do you want to know."

His brows rise. "Can't I get to know you?"

The server brings the wine, interrupting our conversation only for me to do a double take at the brand. Because what that man just poured into my glass must be worth three hundred dollars.

"Go on," Vincenzo beckons, and he picks up his glass.

"Drink."

I take a sip. It tastes like heaven but also like money. Lots and lots of money. Swallowing feels like a sin. Still, I muster a gulp.

"And?"

"Good. Very good," I respond.

He smiles. "I'm glad, considering the price."

"You didn't have to order this for me," I say.

"Oh, no, I wanted to," he replies. "Very much."

I'm stunned by his response. I don't understand why he's so kind.

"Why do you want to spend so much money on me?" I ask, suspicious of his motives. "First a dress, now this."

"Is it forbidden to want to help people?" he retorts.

"No," I say, "but ..."

He leans across the table and places his hand on mine. "Then let me help."

He stares into my eyes with a kind of crushing weight I've never experienced before, and I can't look away, no matter how hard I try.

"You were hungry, so let me feed you," he says. "You were cold and wet, so let me offer you clothes."

I want to accept this kindness so desperately, but ... "What do you expect from me?"

People always want *something*. I've been disappointed too much in life to expect anything else.

He pauses, visibly annoyed. "*Nothing.*"

He can't be serious. All this ... in exchange for nothing?

"You're joking, right?" I jest. "There must be something you want from me."

"Is that what you're used to?" he asks. "People asking for something in return?"

It hits a little too close to home, and I pull back my hand.

"I won't ask for anything ..." he says. "But I need you to be honest with me."

I frown, but then the server comes back and asks, "Have you made a choice?"

I stare at the menu, not knowing what I'm allowed to order. Because I can't pay for any of this.

"We'll have the steak," Vincenzo fills in for me. "You're not vegetarian, right?"

I shake my head, and he smiles while the server takes our menus and walks away.

But Vincenzo immediately homes in on me again. "Do you have somewhere to stay?"

I take a big gulp of my wine, almost choking on it.

But he refuses to look away.

"I ..."

"You don't, do you?" he says.

I shake my head. I don't like admitting it, but he already figured it out, judging by the look of pity on his face.

"That's why you were in that alley," he says.

I take another big gulp of wine until my glass is empty. But then I'm instantly reminded of my situation ... and the thing growing inside me that I never really wanted.

I place my hand on my belly, feeling instantly guilty for chugging down that expensive wine.

What am I going to do about this?

When I look up again, his eyes have lowered to where my hand is, and I immediately remove it.

Shit. Did he notice?

The food is brought out and placed in front of us, the smells mouth-watering. I feel almost sick for even wanting to eat it. It's so expensive. I could've bought a week's worth of food for my mom and me just from the cost of this dish.

But I don't live with her anymore.

She made that painfully clear.

I swallow and pick up my fork and knife.

"Go on. Take a bite," Vincenzo says.

I do what he tells me because I don't want to offend him. But the second the steak hits my tongue, it practically melts in my mouth and makes me want to cry.

"Good, right?" he says, smiling contently.

"I've never had something this good."

He cuts into his steak in such a peculiar way that it draws my attention. Veggies and potatoes are also on his plate, but none of them is allowed to touch each other. When he cuts, he puts in the extra effort so that every piece looks exactly the same.

Strange, if you ask me.

But I guess nothing is strange anymore after today.

He takes a small bite and says, "You can have this every day of the week if you like."

My fork clatters onto my plate. "What?"

Vincenzo leans forward and places his hand on top of mine. "I want to offer you a place to stay."

I can't even swallow the second bite. "But why … me?"

He gently caresses the top of my hand, making heat course through my veins. "Because I do not like injustice." He licks his lips. "And you've been dealt too much."

THREE

Vincenzo

She can barely speak without stuttering. "What do you mean?"

But I think she knows exactly what I mean.

I tilt my head. "I want to take you home with me."

"Home ... with you?"

Is it such a preposterous idea? To be taken home by a man like me?

Or is she just scared of what I might do?

I release her hand and take another bite of my steak, swallowing it down. She watches me like a hawk, almost as if she's tempted by the mere idea of coming home with me

31

but too afraid to take the leap.

"You'll have your own room and bath. A key to lock the door." I look up into her beautiful eyes that could haunt my soul if I let them. "I won't bother you... unless you want me to."

A glimmer in her eyes makes it so damn hard to keep the predator in me at bay.

"What's the catch?" she asks after a while.

I cut off another piece of my steak. "There is none."

"But you must gain something from doing this, right?"

She doesn't trust me, and I understand that. We barely know each other.

But she'll become acquainted with me soon enough.

"The opportunity to help someone in need is enough for me," I reply.

She takes another bite of her food. "So you're like ... pretending to be a Robin Hood or something." She snorts at her own comment.

But I don't find it funny. "Yes."

She looks up and swallows with trouble. "You're serious."

"Yes."

She frowns. "So you've got all this money and want to spend it on me?"

"Yes."

I don't know how many more yeses she needs from me to understand my goal.

"Wow." She cuts into her steak and takes another bite.

"Is it that strange for a rich man to want to share his wealth?"

She makes a face. "Well, you're the first rich man I've met who's attempted it."

"Then you've only met bastards," I reply.

She puts her fork and knife down and pushes herself away from the table. "So do you do this often? Randomly help people in need?"

"Only when I find those worthy of giving it to," I respond.

She sure has many questions for a girl plucked from the streets. But I understand. In her precarious position, she must be careful.

It is the exact reason I wanted her off those streets, to begin with.

"So will you accept?" I ask.

She looks up at me for a moment, her cheeks slowly turning red, which she hides behind a veil of hair. "I don't know, I mean my mom, she—"

"Was the reason you were in that alley. No?" I interrupt before she can start making excuses. "She doesn't need you. If your fight was that bad, you deserve a safe space to stay. For now."

She narrows her eyes at me like she can't believe I'm offering this. Like it's some kind of trap. She refuses to touch her food, despite enjoying the taste. I guess it's a bit too much to take in all at once.

I place my card on the table and signal the server. "I'd

like to pay."

"Of course, sir." The server takes my card and quickly swipes it before bringing it back. "Thank you, sir."

I put back my wallet while the girl still looks at me like she can't decide what to do, so I get up and say, "Think about it. Once you've decided, I'll be outside waiting for your answer."

As I walk off, a hand suddenly wraps around my wrist. "Wait."

Her eyes find mine, and for a moment, it feels as though the world around us completely disappears and all that's left is her and me, and the words she's about to speak from that pretty little mouth of hers.

"Yes."

And a wicked smile forms on my face. "Good choice."

***

Emilia

His house is huge. I don't think I could even call it a house. It's like a giant mansion with endless corridors and rooms all around, lavish carpets, expensive leather furniture that looks almost untouched, several big, erotic paintings hanging from the walls, and crystal chandeliers scattered all around. Like a small castle but with a modern take.

I could never imagine visiting a house like this, let alone living in it. I feel like I'm walking inside a museum where you're not allowed to touch anything, that's how squeaky clean it all looks.

Suddenly, my eyes land on a couple of guards standing near two doors. I turn to look behind me. The car is gone, and the door is being closed by a bunch of guards as well.

All of them visibly wearing guns.

And it becomes harder and harder to breathe.

So I was right. This kind of money does come at a price.

Who in the hell have I involved myself with?

"C'mon, I'll show you to your room," Vincenzo says.

Fuck. Too late to turn back now.

I walk behind him, careful not to touch anything for fear I might break his precious things. I don't want to anger a man who's so generously opened his home to me.

Especially when he's got men like that guarding this place.

But I still feel a little uneasy with how simple this all feels. Like it's somehow a trap, and I'm walking straight into it.

I swallow back the nerves as we head up the giant staircase. His footsteps are soft but firm, like a man who knows he's impressive without having to appear aggressive. Dominant but without the overbearing, threatening part.

And I don't know why, but for some reason, just the way he walks makes it hard for me to look anywhere else but at him as he guides me down a set of hallways and into a room.

"This is yours for as long as you'd like," he says, pointing inside. "Go on. Take a look."

I head inside and marvel at the beauty around me, the huge windows in the back with giant black curtains hanging to the side, the bathtub in front of the windows, and the big bed in the middle of the room with black-and-white satin sheets. It's all so perfect I could cry.

"Do you like it?" he asks.

I push away the tears. I don't know what I did to deserve all of this ... and that the cost won't be steep.

"It's gorgeous," I say. "So much more than I could ever ..."

I sigh. I can't even finish the sentence. I just want to look around and bask in all the wealth before it's all taken away again.

I check the room, touching every inch of it like it's precious. A closet to the right is filled to the brim with clothes and shoes, all as beautiful as the dress I'm wearing. The one he bought me.

I walk to the window and stare outside at the beautiful garden underneath with a field filled with flowers. Beautiful, just like this house. Just like him. Almost too beautiful to be real.

Is this all just a wild dream concocted in my mind after falling asleep from pure exhaustion, and will I find myself back in that alley like nothing ever happened?

A cold shiver runs up and down my spine.

Suddenly, two hands land on my shoulders, making me jolt up and down.

"Don't be frightened of me," he muses, his voice soft, almost... seductive. My body erupts into goose bumps.

But it's hard not to be afraid, knowing the kind of power he holds. "Your men wear guns."

"It's for protection," he answers softly.

"Whose?"

He leans in, whispering into my ear, "Mine ... and yours."

I struggle to even breathe at all. He's right there, breathing into the nape of my neck, every hair on my body aware of his presence so close I could feel his aura rub against mine.

"Are you scared?" he whispers.

I suck in a ragged breath. "Maybe."

"I won't harm you," he says. I could listen to his soft and seductive voice for ages, and it still not be long enough.

How is he, a man I barely even met, able to have such an effect on me?

"Who ... who are you?"

"You know my name," he responds. "Ask the right question."

"What do you do to make all of this money?"

"I am the don of the Ricci Mafia family," he says, the words creating a visceral throbbing in my heart.

"A mobster," I say under my breath.

Oh God. I really have gotten myself into some deep shit.

"Yes. But I don't operate like any other mobster." He stares at me through the glass of the window.

"How so?"

"I sell my goods only to the rich and powerful at exorbitant prices and rob them of their wealth." He slides aside a few strands of hair and tucks them behind my ear, exposing my neck. "Their wealth I give to people in need."

"The Robin Hood of the Mafia," I say.

"If you want to call it that," he replies.

And I'm his next altruistic target.

"Does it frighten you?" he asks.

After a while, I shake my head.

"You've seen much worse, haven't you?"

I lower my eyes and gaze at my own belly, which seems so big now that I really know what's been growing inside me all this time while I just thought I was getting fatter.

Even if this man is dangerous, I'm in no position to say no to the things he's offering me. A room, a warm bed, delicious food, a hot shower.

And I definitely want all of those things.

"You can stay here for as long as you like," he says.

I turn around to face him, but it's so hard to look at a face as handsome as his. "What will it cost me?"

He tilts his chin up, and I swallow down the nerves.

Every man is the same. They all want only one thing.

Sex.

And I know how to do that.

I place my hand on his chest, my hand sliding down his

body, but when I reach his belt, he grabs my wrist and stops me.

"Is this what you were forced to do?"

I gasp.

"Is that how you got this?" He places a hand on my belly.

I lean back in shock. "How did you know?"

He snorts. "I've seen you looking at your belly. It's obvious you're pregnant."

I wince at hearing those words out loud again.

"Is that why you were out on the streets?" When I look away, he tilts my chin with a single finger and forces me to look at him. "Answer me, please."

"Yes."

His nostrils flare, and his lips twitch.

"This pregnancy … is it your choice?"

I swallow, not wanting to give the answer to a man I barely even know. But what choice do I even have? I don't want to seem ungrateful.

After a while, I shake my head. "I'm not on the pill. He didn't want to use a condom. Said it would stop the pleasure. I wasn't able to say no."

Vincenzo releases my wrist, and I try to compose myself, but it's hard when faced with a man as impressive and dominant as him. It's like every look, every gaze, every word of his is laced with power. The kind I've never had.

"Thank you," he says. "For your honesty."

I lick my lips and let my eyes travel down his chiseled

face and chest, the buttons of his shirt barely able to contain the pecs hiding behind. It's rare that I meet anyone with such a physique who's also a gentleman. And I don't think I'd even mind it if I had to pay for my stay with body contact.

But he steps back and grabs my hand, bringing it to his lips for a kiss so gentle it takes my breath away.

Until his eyes look up, boring straight into mine. "You do not need to earn your keep … but I do require you to tell me who it was that got you pregnant."

I gulp. "Um …"

His grip on my hand grows stronger. "The truth, Emilia."

"Dean Johnson. He lives downtown. St. Peter's Street thirty-five, upper floor apartment number twenty-six."

His eyes twitch again, and a fire grows inside them. One I haven't seen before.

"Thank you."

He presses another kiss on top of my hand and releases me, then turns around and waltzes off. And I just know I set off a ticking time bomb that'll be impossible to defuse.

FOUR

Vincenzo

That look of hatred she gave her own belly … that's what drives me mad.

I've seen that look from so many women, and nothing ever comes close to fixing it.

Except one thing.

Vengeance.

The car pulls up to the place she mentioned. An old, beaten-down apartment building that doesn't seem to ever get cleaned. I get out of the car, and the immediate stench of piss makes bile rise in my throat.

I swallow it down and check my watch.

Five minutes, in and out. Should be enough. Though I'm more than willing to spend my precious time on her ... I am far from willing to spend any on the likes of the man who did this to her.

I head inside. The elevator is malfunctioning, so I take the staircase instead. It smells rank in here, and the sun barely penetrates through the small windows in the walls. Just the kind of place where I'd picture a dude who'd stick his dick inside a girl who doesn't want it would live.

Once I'm up to the floor this Dean Johnson lives at, my heartbeat slowly picks up as I count down all the numbers on each door until I reach his.

I pause in front of the door and listen to the sounds coming from behind it.

Lots of screeching women. Moaning. Sloshing sounds like someone is vicariously stirring through some homemade butter. Not the good kind.

My nostrils begin to twitch again like they always do when my blood begins to boil.

Is this motherfucker busy with tricking yet another woman?

I knock on the door, then grab one of the tissues from my pocket and clean my fingers.

The mere thought of touching his things is disgusting, but I don't want to alert the rest of the people living in this building by just breaking into his place.

I tuck the tissue back in my pocket and wait.

The sound of footsteps hurriedly shutting off whatever was moaning tells me it was a recording.

"Just a minute," the voice calls.

I don't hear any other people or footsteps as he rushes to the door.

It's opened slightly, and he peeks at me through the slit. "What do you want?"

Within seconds, I've fished my gun from my pocket and shove it into the opening, putting a foot between so he can't close it on me. "Move. Now."

The man's eyes widen, and he immediately steps back. I walk inside, breathing through my mouth because of the stench. There's half-eaten food and unwashed clothes everywhere, the bane of my existence. Triggers all around, but the biggest of them all is the guy's face.

"What do you want? I don't have anything. No cash, nothing," he squeals.

"Sit your ass down," I growl, shoving him into the couch he was just on. I can still see the cum stain on the fake leather, as well as on his cheap pants.

"Please, just take anything you want," he says, holding up his hands.

"What did you do to Emilia?" I ask.

He frowns, visibly confused. "Who?"

"Emilia!" I shove the gun further into his forehead. "Long black hair. Cupid lips. Pretty girl." I seethe with rage. "Pregnant."

His pupils dilate.

So he does know her.

"Pregnant?" he mutters, shaking his head. "No, that's

43

not possible. I—"

"So you do remember." I pull the safety off the trigger.

"No, I don't remember shit." He's gotten pretty pissed off at that comment, it seems. "Get the fuck out of my house."

I pull away the gun, only to shoot his foot.

He shrieks in agony as blood gushes out.

"You fucking shot me!" he growls.

I point it at his crotch. "Yeah, and your dick is next if you don't answer me."

Panic seeps into his eyes. "Okay, okay, I knew her, yes!"

"How?"

"We had sex," he splutters out.

"And?" I grit.

"She should've been on the pill."

"She wasn't," I growl back. "And you refused a condom, didn't you?"

Sweat drops roll down his forehead as he cowers in the corner of his couch. "I'm sorry! I'm sorry! I didn't mean to—"

"Don't," I say through gritted teeth. "Not to me."

And I grab him by the collar and drag him out of this disgusting cave of a house and all the way down the staircase and out of the building, throwing him in the back of the car.

"Shield up. Lock him in place," I tell my driver. "We're going for a ride."

***

44

He's been kicking and screaming his lungs out in the back of my car for twenty minutes. To no avail, of course. This car is soundproof for a reason, as well as impervious to any kind of attack, whether from the inside or the outside.

That's normal when it comes to my line of work.

But my usual victims are rich and sophisticated, not these boneheaded disgusting little perverts.

But for her, I will do the work.

I will stomach the stench of this filth as long as it takes just so I can fix what he broke.

Repairing small inches of this world is what I do best. Just picking up one broken porcelain teacup and gluing all the pieces together again with golden paint until it's brand new and sparkling even brighter than it ever did before it was destroyed.

And she … she will fucking shine when I am done polishing her.

"Let me out!" Dean squeals from the back.

My hand forms a fist at the thought of this fucker touching her, let alone forcing her to have sex without protection. I was this close to just shooting his dick off and letting that be his punishment for his crime.

He should feel lucky he's in the back of my car instead of buried underground.

When the car finally stops, I hop out and walk up to my guards at the front door. "Bring the fucker inside. Cuff him. Make sure he can't do any harm."

"Yes, sir," they both reply, and I head inside. "Is she still there?" I ask one of the maids, who nods.

I walk upstairs, skipping a few steps, carefully placing my feet only on the spots I usually walk on, and go straight to her room. When I open the door, she's seated down, brushing her hair in front of the mirror, still wearing the beautiful dress I bought for her.

"Vincenzo," she mutters, her eyes glimmering as though she's surprised to see me. "You're back."

I walk up to her, gazing at her beauty through the mirror. "You look gorgeous."

She blushes, and I know, even if she were to deny it, my words obviously have an effect on her. "Thank you."

"I have a gift for you."

I snap my fingers, and the men waiting behind the door bring Dean inside.

Emilia's pupils dilate, and she jolts up, knocking over the seat.

"Dean…" she mutters as the guard shoves him inside. "What are you …?"

My guard prods him with the gun, and her eyes home in on the bloodied hole in his shoe.

"Oh my God …" she murmurs, her hand propped in front of her mouth.

She almost approaches him until my guard takes off the safety of his gun. In the middle of the room, she stands frozen.

I walk up to her and place my hands on her shoulders.

"What did you do?" she asks, her voice unsteady. "You shot him?"

I whisper into her ear, "He hurt you, didn't he?"

She doesn't answer, but her hand slowly slides down to her belly.

"Exactly," I say.

"No, I didn't do it on purpose," Dean says.

"You didn't want to use a condom," she says.

"I thought you were on the pill," Dean stammers, sweating like crazy.

"I told you I wasn't," she replies, her voice getting more and more unhinged. Angered. Just like I anticipated.

Dean stares at her belly. "So it's true? You're pregnant?"

She nods, and I can feel her muscles coil up with rage.

"But I don't want a freaking kid," he mutters. "I don't even know you."

My fingers dig into her skin. "You don't even know her? When you stuck your d—"

Emilia's hand on mine silences me. "I don't really know him either."

I frown, confused.

"We just had … sex," she mutters.

"And I fucking paid for it," he adds.

Paid for it?

"You accepted it," Dean says. "You knew this could happen."

"Enough," I say, and I waltz toward the guard, take his gun from him, and point it at Dean's head. "You've given her enough pain."

"Stop." Emilia's voice prevents me from pulling the trigger.

I turn to look at her.

"This isn't right," she says.

Dean whimpers in fear.

"He hurt you," I say.

"I know …" She gazes down at her belly. "But it was my choice to let him pay for sex. I chose to do that. Not him." She averts her eyes, unable to look at either of us. "I needed the money. Badly."

My nostrils flare, and I lower my gun. Then I nod at the guard so he leaves us alone.

"Come here," I say.

After a while, I hear her steps behind me.

I turn and place the gun in her hands.

"This was my gift to you … I'll leave it up to you to decide his fate."

She holds it with both hands, almost as if it's too heavy of a burden for her to carry.

"Please," Dean mutters. "I didn't mean for this to happen. I never thought it would. I swear, I will do whatever you want." He's crying now. "Please, don't kill me."

She stares at him, her fingers latching onto the gun like it's her last lifeline, and all she wants to do is end her own misery.

But then she chucks it away.

"Bad choices made me pregnant," she growls. "But they

won't turn me into a murderer."

"Thank you," Dean splutters with drool and tears all over his face.

"I never want to see your face near me or my mother's house ever again. Do you hear me?"

He nods a few times.

She's much more forgiving than I expected.

And much more merciful than I would have been.

Through gritted teeth, I tell Dean, "Leave."

And he runs off, skittering away like a bug I was just about to squash.

Emilia was generous enough to let him keep his life. More generous than I ever would've been if I was in her position.

I turn to face her, but she seems unsteady on her feet. Just before she falls, I grab her and hold her against me. "Whoa. Are you okay?"

She breathes a few sighs. "That was … rough."

"I'm sorry if I ended up hurting you too now," I say. "I merely wanted to offer you a chance at payback."

I can feel her swallow against my chest, and it makes all kinds of dirty images float through my head.

"But you didn't take it."

"I don't want to be a monster," she says.

What an innocent angel. Precious. Desirable.

She looks up at me with those same doe-eyes she gave me when I first saw her, and something about them unfurls a deep-seated desire that I'd kept buried for a long time.

"But I want to thank you," she mutters. "For bringing him here. For making him face what he did."

"What I do will never be enough to fix what he broke," I say, my fingers slowly twirling around her hair, desperate to touch her, even when I know I shouldn't.

"You've already given me so much," she says, licking her lips, drawing so much attention to those luscious lips of hers.

I tilt her chin with my finger and lean in. "You deserve so much more."

And without a second thought, I press my lips on hers.

Vincenzo

I can't stop myself any longer. I must have her. Even if I know it's wrong, even if I told myself I never would.

I never fall for the people I help. But I've never kissed one of them either. And definitely never someone so sweet and innocent … and kissable.

And good God, the moment my lips landed on hers, I knew I was in deep. Because fuck me, kissing her is as if sin itself has entered my veins. And now that I've had a taste, I want more, so much more.

But she suddenly pulls back and stares at me, confused.

Shame rolls through my body.

I shouldn't have done that.

I told her she didn't have to earn her keep, and I meant it.

But damn … I've wanted nothing more since I met her than to kiss those lips and make her body mine.

Her lips pout, and for a moment, it feels as though the earth has stopped revolving. Until she suddenly wraps her hands around my neck and smashes her lips on mine.

And fuck me, I've lost my will to fight my own conscience instantly.

Our kiss is heated and aggressive. I groan against her mouth and claim her lips like they've always belonged to me. My tongue dips out to break them open and force my way inside, licking the roof of her mouth.

She tastes like heaven and everything I've longed for.

But she's here to be helped, not to be used.

"We should stop," I mutter between kisses.

"Should we?" she murmurs.

I pull back to gaze at her swollen, red lips. "You don't have to do this."

She licks her lips, pressing up against me until my cock hardens against her thighs. "I know …"

When her hands slide down my chest, all the way across my abs, my cock throbs with need. And as her fingers land on my package, I grasp her wrist and say, "I meant it when I said I don't need payment."

She grins. "I remember … but I'm still grateful."

I push her back against the wall and pin her against it. "I

don't *need* you to be grateful. I need you …"

"You need me to … what?" she repeats, gazing up at me with those starstruck eyes, those delicious lips begging me to kiss them.

"I need you …" I rasp, dangerously close. "I fucking need you to beg."

Her lips part, and I can see the shock riddle on her face.

But I can't fucking let myself go. Not until she gives me the one word I need.

Her lips part, her cheeks glowing red with embarrassment. "Please."

Fuck.

That's the one.

I immediately slam my lips on hers, not giving a shit if it's wrong. I know I'm not supposed to take from those who have nothing left to give, but I can't stop myself. The moment I laid eyes on her, I knew I was in trouble.

Those looks she gave me, the way her hand fits so perfectly in mine, the way I've felt so fiercely protective over this girl, despite only knowing her for a day, it's all starting to make sense now.

I'm stricken by desire, completely corrupted by it, as my hands roam freely across her body, her tits, ripping the dress down.

She moans into my mouth, but I cover her mouth with mine as I fondle her perky tits, flicking my thumbs across her nipples until they harden.

"Fuck, I want you," I groan against her lips. "So badly."

"Then take it," she murmurs back as my mouth drags a line down her neck. "Take all of me."

Her words drive me mad with lust as I press kisses on her shoulders and let my tongue slide down her skin, all the way to her tits, taking one into my mouth and sucking hard.

I don't want her just because she's offering.

I want her because it's forbidden.

Because she's the one I should be helping, and I want nothing more than to take everything she has left to give.

"Tell me to stop," I say, kissing every inch of her skin.

"No," she replies.

I kiss her so hard we're both out of breath. "Tell me." I tug at her lip with my teeth and leave a mark. "Now or I swear to God, I'll fuck you every fucking day of the week until you can no longer stand on two feet."

She'd better deny me, shove me away, slap me.

Because if she doesn't, I'm ready to stake my claim.

"Fuck …" she whispers, licking her lips. "Yes."

***

Not one second does he wait. He immediately grabs me by the ass and lifts me up, kissing me like his life depends on it. Groping me, he plants me down on the dressing table and shoves aside everything in his way without ever taking his lips off mine.

He touches me in all the right places, and I lean back against the mirror as he plants kisses down my sternum and slides across my nipples. My body burns with desire for him. His hand dives between my legs, rubbing my clit right through the fabric of my panties, and good God, does he know how to find it.

"Tell me how badly you want it," he groans, sliding his finger up and down, toying with me.

"Oh God, I want you so much," I mewl.

"Is that why you threw yourself at me so carelessly?"

I nod, bucking my hips into the palm of his hand.

He's been on my mind ever since he left the house. Everywhere I went in this room, his scent lingered. All I could think about was the way he leaned in so close that I could almost kiss him. And when I wanted to pay him, he didn't even accept it, despite the fact that I could feel the tension between us.

And it's given me nothing but more wantonness.

God, this man's lips are too sinful to be real. And the way his fingers slip up and down my wet panties make me want to rub myself against him.

I've never craved a man this much before.

Then again, I've never met a man quite like him.

So handsome I could die … and so vicious he could almost make me kill.

But I'm glad I didn't because none of this would've

happened. His hands wouldn't be all over my ass and pussy, and my lips wouldn't be on his neck, desperate for more.

"You were right … there is one thing I want from you," he groans into my ear.

"Tell me," I reply.

He tugs aside my panties and shoves a few fingers into my pussy, making me gasp. "I want your wetness all over my fingers. Now."

I moan out loud when he begins to thrust, alternating harsh with gentle, driving me mad. Between thrusts, his thumb rolls around on my most sensitive part until my eyes almost roll just as hard.

"Yes, that's it. Give me your biggest orgasm right fucking now, Emilia."

Just his voice alone pushes me over the edge, and I come harder than I ever have before.

Jesus Christ, this man knows how to work a clit.

"Good girl," he whispers into my ear, making me whimper.

I was never the girl for praise … until today.

He opens his belt buckle and tears it off, then wraps it around my hands.

"Wow," I mutter.

He raises a brow. "Scared?" The belt is tied firmly.

"No," I lie. I've seen and done much in my time, but it's not what he does that scares me … it's who he is. What he *could* do.

But I trust him.

After all, he did bring Dean to my feet and made him cry.

Vincenzo went through all that trouble just to give me what no one else could give.

He likes me.

And I think that's what frightened me the most when he first came to me in that alley, promising me something I never thought anyone ever would: Another chance.

He licks his lips. "I smell a lie."

I giggle, but he swiftly grabs my face and sticks his tongue in my mouth, claiming me with fervor. "You won't be giggling like that when I'm done with you."

He rips off my panties in one go, making me squeal into his mouth. Then he pulls down his zipper and takes out his cock, which is so big it makes my eyes widen. Oh God. Am I going to regret this?

"Spread your legs for me, Emilia," he says, stepping back only to look at my pussy, his tongue dipping out to lick his lips. He pulls out a condom from his pocket and rips it open, wrapping it over his length. His fingers trail the tip of his dick as he eyes me down with hungry eyes. "Show me how much you want it."

My fingers splay behind my back, tortured that I can't touch myself, let alone him, to do something about this lust coursing through my body.

"Fuck," I murmur. "Give it to me."

With a smug grin, he steps forward, cock hard and dripping with pre-cum. I swallow away the lump in my throat when I realize he's much bigger up close than I anticipated.

Fuck, this is going to get dirty.

He grips my thighs, nails digging into my skin as he leans forward and whispers into my ear, "Beg."

"Please ..."

Not one second does he wait as he thrusts inside to the hilt. My mouth makes an o-shape, a strangled moan escaping my throat as his length throbs inside me.

His lips are on me in an instant, claiming even more raunchy kisses as he begins riding me harder and harder, deepening each stroke. My hands are helplessly searching behind my back to hold on to something, but all I have is the metal clasp of the belt, pricking into my skin.

"Fuck, you're so wet for me," he groans, plunging in again and again until my eyes almost roll into the back of my head.

"That's it, Emilia, give me another orgasm," he growls as his thumb moves down between my legs, rubbing my clit until my legs begin to quake.

"It's so big," I mumble. "So full."

"And you'll be even fuller when I shoot my load deep inside this pussy," he replies.

I gasp in shock, but he swiftly covers my mouth again, burying himself inside me until his balls tighten against me.

"Fuck, I'm going to explode inside you and fill you to the brim, and you're going to come just from my cock alone," he groans.

"Yes," I mewl with desire as he thrusts so hard the dressing table begins to quake.

His thumb expertly rolls around my clit until I'm delirious with need, my body leaning into his hand and cock, desperate for more. His lips are on my sternum and breasts, sucking at one of my nipples while the other is being tugged.

And I moan out loud as I explode into bliss, another orgasm making all my muscles twitch and coil.

Right then, he moans along with me, thrusting in deep as his cock begins to throb with heat.

After a while, he brings his lips to my mouth and kisses me so gently I'm overcome with a sensation I've rarely ever felt: love.

Fuck. I've really fallen hard for a guy I barely even know.

"My God …" I mutter.

"That good, huh?" he muses.

I nod as he slowly pulls out of me and takes off the condom, chucking it into the bin next to the dressing table.

Then he walks to the bathroom and washes his hands, and it makes me frown, confused. Who would do that the second they were done with sex?

"Why … did you wash your hands?" I ask.

"A habit," he explains. "Autism."

Oh wow. I hadn't thought of that. But it makes sense, in the bigger picture, now that I think about it.

"Does that unsettle you?"

I quickly shake my head. "No. I'm more curious than

ever, actually."

He smiles, and the warmth that radiates off him makes me feel like I'm on cloud nine.

I'm still sitting on the table, wrists still tied, body numb with pleasure, and I just watch and admire him from afar. "I wish I could've had this sooner," I mumble. "Maybe then I wouldn't have—"

He places a finger on my lips as he treads close again, standing between my thighs, his cock still half-hard from the bout of sex. "You can."

My pupils dilate.

"I told you this wasn't for payment," he says. "I want you to stay with me."

"With you?" It sounds too good to be true.

"Be mine."

The gravity of his words slowly sink in as I stare into his eyes, but there's no lie to be found.

"Only if you want to," he adds as he releases my wrists from their bonds.

I don't even know how to respond as tears well up in my eyes. If I could stay here, forever, in this home, with this man ... it would be the end of all my struggles. And the beginning of something new and exciting. "Am I dreaming?" I ask, completely overwhelmed with the possibilities.

He chuckles and caresses my cheeks. "If you are ... let me make it come true."

#

Vincenzo

Days later

Sitting on a small bench, I vigorously tap my foot, annoyed at how long it's taking those nurses to help Emilia. She'd better not be in too much pain, or else there will be hell to pay for this clinic.

I look around at all the women waiting their turn. It can't be easy being here. And I admire each and every one for being brave enough to come, despite the picketers trying to chase them off outside.

I grab my cup and take a sip of water, nearly squashing it

with my hands when I hear the noise outside blasting over the gentle music coming from the speakers.

The woman working behind the counter, registering all the information of the women who come here, puts in a pair of earplugs and types away into her computer. She must be sick and tired of all those goddamn annoying people out there.

Maybe, when I'm done destroying the rich and feeding the poor, I'll focus on them next.

Suddenly, the door in the back opens, and a nurse steps out. She walks toward me, bringing me a few papers. "She asked me to give you this."

Her accent catches me off guard.

It always takes me a while to get used to it when I cross state lines. Sometimes it's simple to forget.

"How is she?" I ask.

"Still recovering. You can go visit her if you want to."

I don't wait another second and put down my cup so I can be with her. I know Emilia needs someone now, more than ever before, and if I can be that person for her, it'd be my honor.

I head inside the recovery room, where she's lying in a bed, her eyes turned away from the door, away from the world.

Tucking my hands into my pocket, I say, "Hey."

Emilia wipes away her tears before turning to look at me. "Hey."

"How do you feel?"

"Shitty." She snorts and laughs, then cries some more.

I reach for her hand and squeeze. "Are you upset it's over?"

She shakes her head. "No. I just feel so … guilty for being so relieved that it's gone."

I smile and lean in to press a kiss to her cheek. "Don't feel guilty. You were not ready."

"No, I wasn't," she replies. "And I didn't want Dean's baby. I never did."

My nostrils flare just from the sound of his name. "Do you want me to end him? Because I will if you've changed your mind."

Her pupils dilate. "No, no, no. It was my choice to let him pay to have sex with me. We needed the money, and Mom said—"

"Mom?" I raise a brow.

She blushes and averts her eyes. "She … was the one who taught me how to sell my body."

"*Sell* your body?" I repeat, my blood turning into pure rage.

"She said that it would make me useful," she adds. "That I could earn my stay."

Fuck.

It takes every ounce of restraint in me not to waltz out of this clinic right now and go find me that woman's head.

"She was your mother," I say through gritted teeth. "And you're telling me she sold her daughter for cash?"

Emilia nods. "We didn't have the money to pay rent or

food, and no one would hire her while she was on drugs."

"On drugs?" I'm almost spitting fire by now.

She licks her lips. "I didn't touch them because of the way they made her behave."

"I'm glad you didn't," I tell her. "Drugs are the worst kind of thing to do to your own body."

"I know … I just wish she would've appreciated all my effort instead of kicking me out."

I grab her chin and make her look at me. "Did she ever hurt you?"

Her face contorts. "Often."

It seems hard to admit.

But it's the kind of detail I won't ever forget.

"Did she ever love you?" I ask.

Tears well up in her eyes. "I don't think so. I was born … only because she didn't have the means to end it before." She swallows. "That's why I didn't want this." She touches her belly. "I'm sorry," she murmurs, her muscles tightening as a wave of pain hits her.

"Don't. Don't apologize." I press another deep kiss to her forehead. "Stop beating yourself up. Rest now."

She breathes a sigh of relief, and as the last tear rolls down her cheeks, a grin spreads on my cheeks.

Because I will not rest … until Emilia has gotten everything she's owed.

**

Emilia

A few days later

I can never get used to being driven around in an expensive car by an actual chauffeur. It feels like I'm living in an alternate reality. One where this man chose me to be his, and I'm continuously swept away into the beautiful darkness surrounding him.

He loves me like he's known me his entire life, and when I'm with him, it feels like this for me too. Deep inside my heart, I can feel him ... keeping the beat going.

Every time I look at him, my heart flutters, and my body fills with heat at the promise of what he's going to do later.

He already gave me a hint.

His belt ... flicked into his hand.

I swallow at the thought of his tongue right there between the crevice of my thighs.

Good God, this man has swallowed me whole, and I'm enjoying every second of it.

He's already done so much for me, and I don't think I can ever repay him.

Not that he wants me to.

He'd probably throw anything I'd try to give him right back at me. That's the kind of love I've found, and it makes me feel like I'm the luckiest girl alive.

The car comes to a stop in the middle of what I'd call the slums of this city, and it's only when I look out the window that I realize where we are. My eyes widen at the sight of my own house.

"This is where you used to live, right?" Vincenzo asks.

I nod, but it barely registers.

I remember telling him about my previous home ... I just never thought I'd actually visit this place again.

The driver steps out and opens our door, and suddenly, I feel frozen to my seat.

"Go on," Vincenzo eggs me on.

With his nudge, my legs cave, and I step out, my whole body shivering with despair.

Vincenzo stands behind me and places his hands on my shoulder, grounding me, reminding me that I'm here with him now, safe.

"Your mother's inside. Do you want to see her?"

I vigorously shake my head. "No. Never again." Rage coils my muscles. "She made me suffer so much."

His fingers dig into my skin. "Did she hurt you?"

I swallow down the lump in my throat. "Many times."

"Physically? Emotionally? Psychologically?"

I nod at all three. She was the worst kind of mother anyone could ever wish for.

It's also one of the reasons I don't want to be one to a child I never wanted.

No child deserves to live like I did, to be born into a world that despises you.

"Do you think she deserves you in her life?" he asks.

I shake my head, emblazoned by my own hatred for her after she kicked me out.

Vincenzo leans in, whispering into my ear, "Then take it from her." He holds up a match in front of my face while he tucks something into my hands.

My eyes slowly lower to look at the item. A wrapped box with a wire at the end.

Vincenzo lights the match.

My soul gasps at the thought, but I still grasp the match.

Could I do it? Would it hurt or would it make me smile?

"Do it." His tongue licks the ream of my ear. "Burn. It. Down."

My hand rises as though possessed by the mere possibility of making her suffer the way she made me suffer, of making her feel the same kind of burn I felt when they scorched that living thing out of my belly.

The match is dropped right onto the wire. And I chuck it at the windows, smashing them. The explosion is almost instant.

A shriek goes off, a siren's call to my heart.

I once thought I could go back …

Not anymore.

And as a wicked smile forms on my lips, a fire erupts inside the house, flames licking at the ceiling, devouring the place and all its dark, depraved memories whole.

Just like my purity.

Burn. It. Down.

THANK YOU

FOR READING!

Thanks so much for reading BURN! I hope you enjoyed. This story was a short prelude into SICK BOYS, a Dark Bully RH/Why Choose Romance. This story features the mother (h) and father (H) of the leading lady.

You can also stay up to date of new books via my website: www.clarissawild.com

I'd love to talk to you! You can find me on Facebook: www.facebook.com/ClarissaWildAuthor, make sure to click LIKE.

You can also join the Fan Club:
www.facebook.com/groups/FanClubClarissaWild and talk with other readers!

Enjoyed this book? You could really help out by leaving a review on Amazon and Goodreads. Thank you!

ALSO BY CLARISSA WILD

Dark Romance

Sick Boys & Evil Boys

Beast & Beauty Duet

Debts & Vengeance Series

Dellucci Mafia Duet

The Debt Duet

Savage Men Series

Delirious Series

Indecent Games Series

The Company Series

FATHER

New Adult Romance

Fierce Series

Blissful Series

Ruin

Rowdy Boy & Cruel Boy

Erotic Romance

The Billionaire's Bet Series

Enflamed Series

Unprofessional Bad Boys Series

Visit Clarissa Wild's website for current titles.

www.clarissawild.com

ABOUT THE AUTHOR

Clarissa Wild is a New York Times & USA Today Bestselling author of Dark Romance and Contemporary Romance novels. She is an avid reader and writer of swoony stories about dangerous men and feisty women. Her other loves include her hilarious husband, her cutie pie son, her two crazy but cute dogs, and her ninja cat that sometimes thinks he's a dog too. In her free time, she enjoys watching all sorts of movies, playing video games, reading tons of books, and cooking her favorite meals.

Want to be informed of new releases and special offers? Sign up for Clarissa Wild's newsletter on her website www.clarissawild.com.

Visit Clarissa Wild on Amazon for current titles.

Printed in the USA
CPSIA information can be obtained
at www.ICGtesting.com
CBHW012121031223
2344CB00004B/135

9 798223 130420